2-14-07 mo

The Tutti-Frutti Case

Starring
The Four Doctors of Goodge

by **Harry Allard**

illustrated by **James Marshall**

Prentice-Hall, Inc. Englewood Cliffs, N.J.

for Philip Holman Proctor
H.A.

for Dr. Mary Elizabeth Devine
J.M.

10   9   8   7   6   5   4   3   2   1

Printed in the United States of America • J

Prentice-Hall International, Inc., London
Prentice-Hall of Australia, Pty. Ltd., North Sydney
Prentice-Hall of Canada, Ltd., Toronto
Prentice-Hall of India Private Ltd., New Delhi
Prentice-Hall of Japan, Inc., Tokyo

Library of Congress Cataloging in Publication Data

Allard, Harry.
  The tutti-frutti case.

  SUMMARY: Four private eyes investigate a plot to
keep everyone in Washington, D.C., from eating their ice cream.
  I. Marshall, James, 1942–   ill. II.   Title.
PZ7.A413Tu   [E]   74-20912
ISBN 0-13-933200-6

Flop! It all began in the back of a crowded bus when a swan dropped her tutti-frutti ice cream cone and began to cry. It was the *fourth* cone she had dropped that day. No! it was just too provoking.

Glurp! At that very moment in another city someone was crying her eyes out on a park bench. Boohoo! A spilled hot fudge sundae lay at her feet. It was the *eighth* spilled hot fudge sundae of the day. She cried and cried.

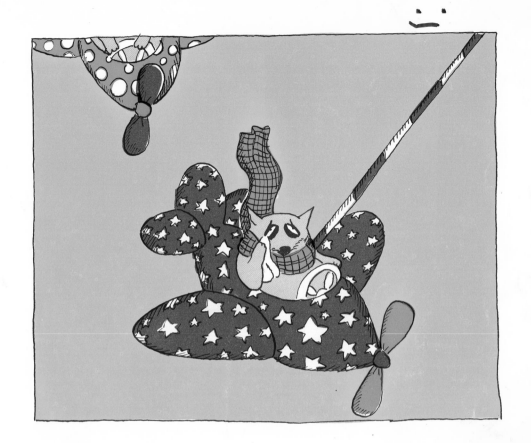

Fff . . . ! At the same time in an amusement park a raccoon was dabbing his little eyes with a tissue. His orange popsicle had simply melted away before his very eyes—before he had even had a chance to take a single bite of it. It was a very sad sight.

Whatever could be the matter? Sundaes, sodas, milkshakes, ice cream cones, and

popsicles were melting and tumbling over right and left, everywhere. And everyone everywhere was crying his eyes out too.

Everyone, that is, except two strange people who lived in a large, dark, spooky old house that smelled of spoiled cabbage leaves and of rotten eggs. *They* weren't crying. Far from it! In fact they were laughing.

"Ginger," hissed a very mean-sounding voice, "push the button down that makes it melt. Hee-hee! Hee-hee!"

"Roger! Woodrow," rasped the second very mean-sounding voice; and they both shrieked with hair-raising laughter: "Ha-ha!"

The country-wide panic caused by the ice-cream problem finally reached the White House itself. Mr. President's very favorite dessert, baked Alaska, had melted right on his plate at a dinner of state.

"This is a case for The Four Doctors of Goodge," barked the President. He took the telephone from its hiding place under the yoyo box, and dialed a secret number: GO-000-04.

Gaston, Gaylord, Garfield, and Skipper Goodge left for Washington, D.C. the very next day in their private train. A crying President and a weeping crowd met them at the station.

As The Four Doctors of Goodge were being driven to their hotel, they saw nothing but sad, tear-stained faces lining the streets and boulevards of the capital.

"This can only be the work of one man," Skipper Goodge said, scratching his chin. "Yes, yes, yes," his brothers Gaston, Gaylord, and Garfield Goodge agreed.

Gaston, Gaylord, Garfield, and Skipper

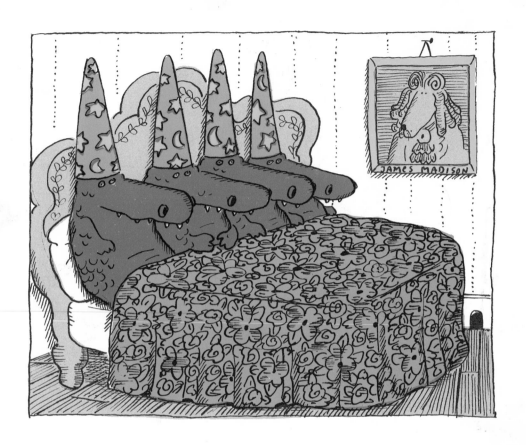

Goodge put on their thinking caps. "We must find a way to tempt him away from his hideout to find out what he is up to," Gaston said.

"But how?" Gaylord asked.

"With food," Skipper Goodge replied.

At the suggestion of The Four Doctors of Goodge, the President threw a party. The menu was unusual. The Four Doctors of Goodge knew who would come.

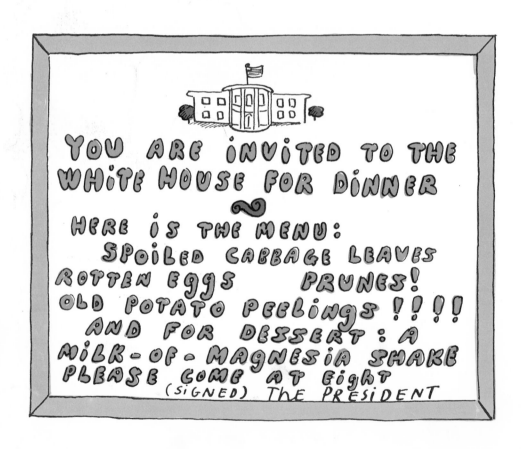

At eight o'clock sharp a sleek shiny limousine driven by a large gray rat drove up to the front door of the White House. A strange-looking pair got out; their mouths were watering. It was easy to see that they were in disguise.

As the spooky couple in funny clothes had seconds, thirds and even fourths of the tasty garbage, The Four Doctors of Goodge were busy tracking down the hideout.

Their Geiger counter, which they had tuned in to pick up the scent of spoiled cabbage leaves and rotten eggs, had led them to

a strange house. Suddenly the Geiger counter
began ticking wildly.

"We're here," Skipper Goodge whispered to his brothers, "Shhh . . . "

Ever so softly, The Four Doctors of
Goodge sneaked into the dark cold house that
reeked of spoiled cabbage leaves and rotten

eggs. They tiptoed through room after room.

In a room, all by itself, they found an amazing machine. It had flashing lights. It had buttons and levers. It made funny gurgling sounds. "Aha!" Skipper Goodge whispered. "Just what I suspected all along: Woodrow Weasel has invented an ice-cream destroying machine."

The Four Doctors of Goodge set to work rewiring the crazy-looking contraption so that it would work backwards. Gaston pulled and Gaylord pushed. Garfield hammered and Skipper fiddled with the dials. Then they left, as quietly as they had entered.

It wasn't until early the next morning that the sleek shiny limousine returned to the dark cold house. Throwing off his disguise, Woodrow Weasel hissed to his faithful companion Ginger Jackal, "What a tasty dinner, Ginger." And throwing off her wig, Ginger rasped in agreement.

  "But now," giggled Woodrow Weasel, "to work, Ginger!" The fiend rubbed his furry paws together in delight.

  "Roger! Woodrow," Ginger Jackal screamed. They scurried off to the laboratory where they kept Woodrow Weasel's greatest invention, The Ice Cream Destroying

Machine. Woodrow was so proud of it. He directed the laser beam; Ginger pushed the buttons down.

But oh! How surprised they both were. The machine was not destroying ice cream. It was *making* ice cream! Ginger and Woodrow gaped at the radar screen thunderstruck.

"We're not making people unhappy, Ginger. We're making everyone happy. happy!"Woodrow Weasel gnashed his false teeth together so hard they fell out. Clunk! And Ginger's wig fell off. Plop!

The two meanies broke down and cried. It was the saddest day of their lives. Worse still, their year's supply of spoiled cabbage leaves and rotten eggs changed into gallons and gallons of vanilla ice cream with little cinnamon hearts.

But it was a great day for the rest of the country. Everyone was smiling, everyone was happy. The President was smiling too. The whole country was grateful to The Four Doctors of Goodge. To honor them, the President had a wonderful new treat named for them. Ten flavors of ice cream, topped with whipped cream smothered in hot fudge, generously sprinkled with chopped walnuts and crowned with four bright red cherries. To this day it's known as

The Goodge Delight.